Baker Makers

Kim Smith

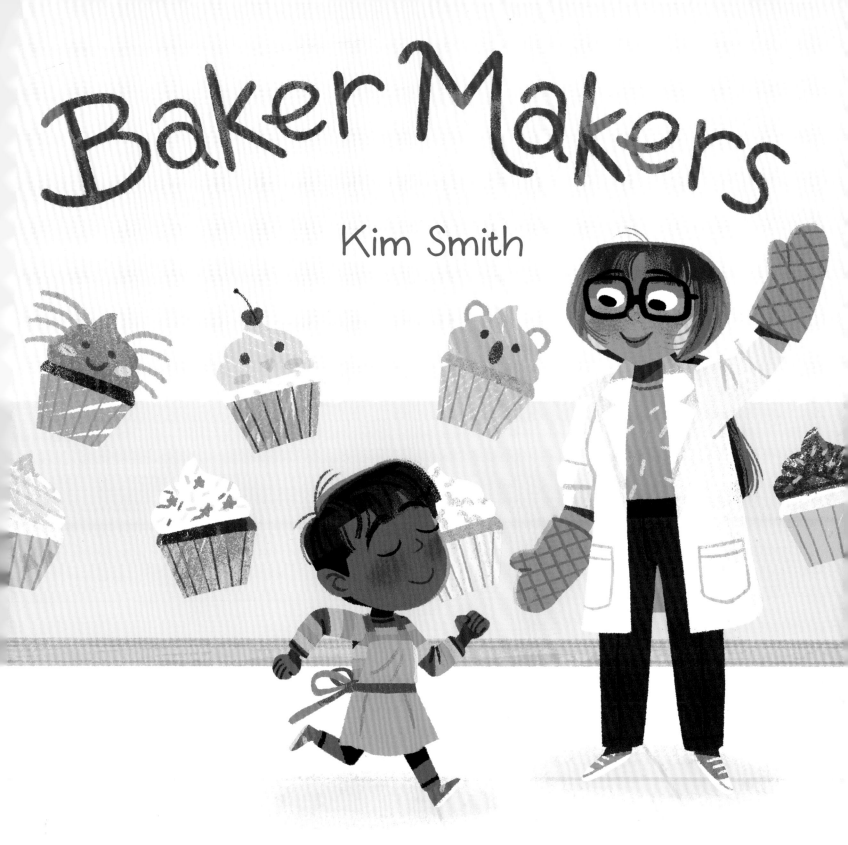

Clarion Books
An Imprint of HarperCollinsPublishers

This week in the Baker Makers Lab, Naveen's class would be making creative cakes.

At home, Naveen had done only a little bit of baking.

But he watched all the baking shows,

pored over pictures, and ate many baked goods.

He was practically a master baker!

Ms. Maple told the class,
"Please start with this basic recipe."

But Naveen wasn't listening.

His cake was going to be better than basic.

First, the students decided on flavor, then shape, and finally frosting and decorations.

Naveen worked hard designing his perfect cake.

My cake will be a chocolate peanut butter log cake!

Mine will be a vanilla rainbow sprinkle cake!

Next, Ms. Maple handed out ingredients and the class started carefully measuring.

For *his* cake, Naveen would rely on instinct.

A little of this,

a lot of that.

Naveen used extra ingredients to
make his cake extra good.

But when he poured the
batter into the pans,
they overflowed.

His classmates' pans looked half empty.
"Big mistake," Naveen said to himself.

Naveen's cake layers seemed to be
taking a very long time to bake.

And they kept growing bigger and bigger.

When it was finally time to take them out . . .

They were burnt on the outside but not quite done in the middle.

Naveen's perfect cake was a perfect disaster.

The other kids came by to see how
Naveen's cake was coming.

"You can fix anything with
frosting," Stevie said.

But the more frosting he added,
the worse it got.

Ms. Maple came by for
a final check.

"An interesting first
attempt!" she said.

When she took a bite,
her face said it all.

It tasted as awful as it looked.

Naveen's classmates tried to comfort him.

After class, Naveen peeked at the other makers' baking stations.

Even though their cakes weren't perfect, they all looked better than his.

The basic recipe!

The next day, Naveen
decided to give the recipe a try.

He measured and combined
the sugar and butter.

He added the eggs, then
the flour and baking powder,
and mixed in the milk.

Finally, he added the flavors:
chocolate and strawberry.

When it came out of the oven,
it was perfectly done!

Smells
delicious!

Naveen realized he didn't have enough cake to create exactly what he had dreamed up.

He might have enough to make a unicorn head, though.

But as he was carving,
Naveen's cake crumbled!

Would this be another
cake disaster?

Unless . . .

By the end of class, Naveen had created something delicious!

Uni-cone Cakes!

Sometimes baking may not work perfectly. But being a great baker maker means rolling with your mistakes.

And sometimes you end up
with something unexpected,
but just as delicious.

Make Your Own
Uni-cone Cakes!

✳ **Adult assistance required** ✳

Naveen made his cake from scratch. But to save time,
you can make uni-cone cakes with a store-bought cake mix!

INGREDIENTS

- 1 box cake mix OR cake made from the basic cake recipe Naveen used (at right)
- 2 cans vanilla frosting (one for making the cake mixture and one for decorating)
- 8 cup-style ice cream cones
- Decorations! (candy, sprinkles, small pretzel sticks)

DIRECTIONS

1. Make the cake following the directions on the box, or if making from scratch, follow Ms. Maple's Basic Cake Recipe. Let the finished cake cool completely.

2. Crumble the cooled cake into fine crumbs in a large bowl.

3. Mix frosting thoroughly into the crumbled cake, one spoonful at a time. The mixture should have enough frosting so it can be molded into a ball, but not so much that it's gooey.

4. Fill each cone to just below the brim with the mixture.

5. Form a ball with ½ cup of the mixture, either with an ice cream scoop or by rolling it with your hands. The ball should be approximately the size of a scoop of ice cream. Place on top of a mixture-filled cone, adhering with a little frosting.

6. Carefully frost the top of the uni-cone cakes— this part is tricky, so ask a grown-up for help!

7. Repeat for the other cones.

8. Decorate your cake-corns with sprinkles and candy! Use the small pretzel sticks for the horns and candy for the ears and eyes.

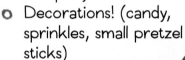

Ms. Maple's Basic Cake Recipe

Ingredients

- 3 cups flour
- 1 tbsp baking powder
- 1 cup unsalted butter, softened
- 2 cups sugar
- 4 large eggs
- 1 tbsp vanilla extract
- 1 cup milk

Directions

1. Preheat oven to 350°F.
2. Grease and flour two 9-inch cake pans
3. Combine flour and baking powder in a large bowl and set aside.
4. Cream butter and sugar together in a medium bowl.
5. Beat in eggs one at a time.
6. Stir in vanilla.
7. Add the wet ingredients to the bowl with the dry ingredients and combine.
8. Add milk and mix.
9. Divide the batter evenly between the two pans.
10. Bake for 30–40 minutes, until a toothpick inserted into the center of the cake comes out clean.

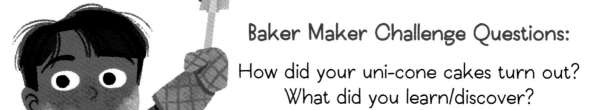

Baker Maker Challenge Questions:

How did your uni-cone cakes turn out?
What did you learn/discover?
What would you try differently next time?

For photos and more cake ideas, projects, and fun experiments, visit Kim Smith's website:
funextras.kimillustration.com

Clarion Books is an imprint of HarperCollins Publishers.

Baker Makers

www.harpercollinschildrens.com

ISBN 978-0-06-324137-4

The artist used Adobe Photoshop to create the digital illustrations for this book.
Design by Phil Caminiti
23 24 25 26 27 RTLO 10 9 8 7 6 5 4 3 2 1

First Edition